W9-DDB-345

HOW YOUR BODY WORKS

Moving Your Body

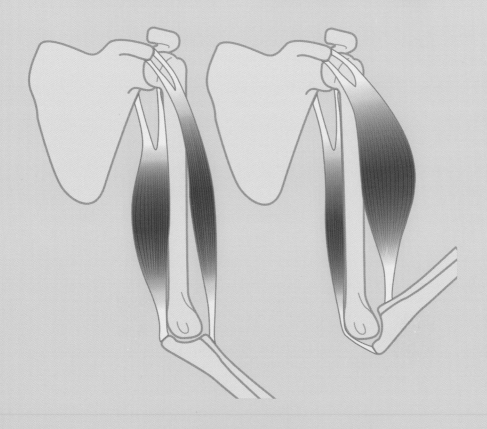

by Philip Morgan

amicus

Published by Amicus
P.O. Box 1329, Mankato, Minnesota 56002

Printed in the United States of America, at Corporate Graphics
in North Mankato, Minnesota

Library of Congress Cataloging-in-Publication Data
Morgan, Philip, 1948 Oct. 16-
  Moving your body / by Philip Morgan.
      p. cm. -- (How your body works)
  Summary: "Discusses the different systems of the body and how they function together to make the body work"--Provided by the publisher.
  Includes index.
  ISBN 978-1-60753-054-1 (library binding)
  1. Human locomotion--Juvenile literature. 2. Human mechanics--Juvenile literature. I. Title.
  QP301.M66 2011
  612.7'6--dc22

                    2009033090

Created by Appleseed Editions Ltd.
Designed by Helen James
Edited by Mary-Jane Wilkins
Artwork by Graham Rosewarne
Picture research by Su Alexander
Consultant: Penny Preston

Photograph acknowledgements
page 4 John Fortunato Photography/Corbis; 5 Rick Gomez/Corbis; 7 Zephyr/Science Photo Library; 9 Scott Camazine/Science Photo Library; 10 Duomo/Corbis; 13 Cory Sorensen/Corbis; 15l Edward Kinsmen/Science Photo Library, r Cordelia Molloy/Science Photo Library; 16 Bob Winsett/Corbis; 18 Ariel Skelley/Corbis; 19 Steve Gschmeissner/Science Photo Library; 20 Adrian Bradshaw/epa/Corbis; 23 D.Roberts/Science Photo Library; 25 Mehau Kulyk/Science Photo Library; 27 GustoImages/Science Photo Library; 29 Living Art Enterprises, LLC/Science Photo Library
Front cover Rick Gomez/Corbis

DAD0037
32010

9 8 7 6 5 4 3 2 1

Contents

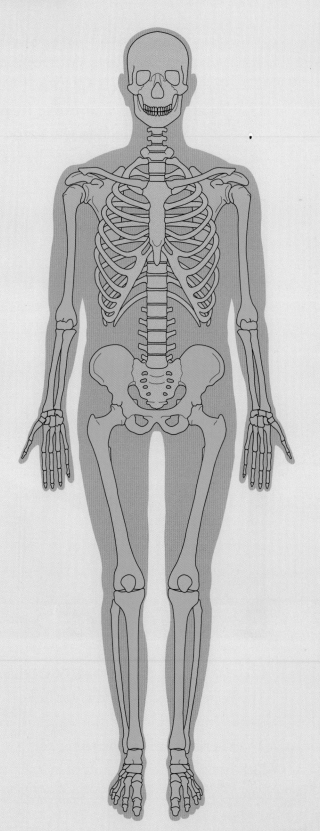

Your Amazing Skeleton

The bones in your skeleton create a strong framework that supports your body. Without it you wouldn't be able to stand up or move. Your skeleton allows you to stand upright and to move in many remarkable ways. Everyone's skeleton has the same pattern and the shape and size of your body are based on the shape of your skeleton.

Hundreds of Movements

The bones of your skeleton are linked by different kinds of joints and muscles. Together they allow you to make hundreds of different movements. At the center of the skeleton is your flexible spine

Soccer players make many different movements.

(see page 20). This holds your head at the top and is anchored to your pelvis at the bottom.

MAKING RED BLOOD CELLS

In the center of some bones, including the bones of the pelvis, spine, breastbone (sternum), and ribs, there is red **bone marrow** that makes the oxygen-carrying red cells of the blood.

Think of all the different movements your body makes. Some of them, such as chewing food, turning your head, or walking, seem to be quite simple. Others, such as swimming, cycling, or playing tennis, are more complicated. Then there are the really difficult movements, such as playing a piano, ballet dancing, or skiing down a mountain.

Joints and Muscles

Many movements would not be possible without joints between your bones and without muscles attached to the bones. There are several types of joints, each one designed to allow you to make a different type of movement. The muscles that move your bones are called skeletal muscles. When a skeletal muscle contracts, it shortens and pulls the bone it is attached to into a new position (see pages 14–15).

Protection

Your skeleton also protects the organs of your body. Your ribs protect your heart and lungs, your **cranium** (the tough upper part of your skull) protects your delicate brain (see pages 22–23), and your pelvis protects your bladder and organs of the lower abdomen.

Swimming is a great all-around activity because it exercises many of the joints and muscles in your body.

Fitting Bones Together

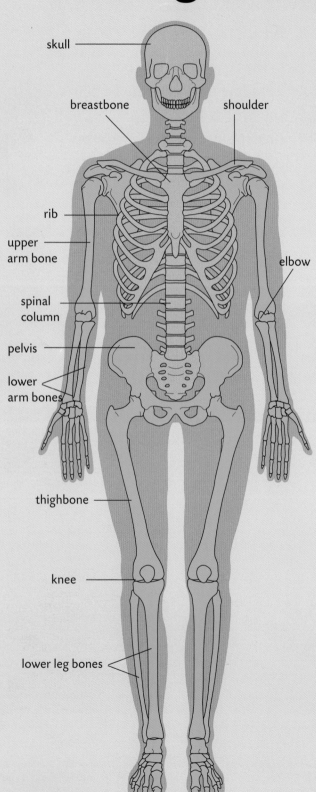

skull

breastbone

shoulder

rib

upper
arm bone

elbow

spinal
column

pelvis

lower
arm bones

thighbone

knee

lower leg bones

A single bone weighs very little, yet bones are as strong as steel and last a long time. They vary in size. The largest is the **femur**, or thighbone. The tiniest is the stirrup, $^3/_{25}$ inch (3 mm) in the middle of the ear. Together with two other tiny bones, it sends sound vibrations from the eardrum to the inner ear.

Shapes of Bones

The shape of a bone depends on what it does. The skull has flat, rounded bones to protect the brain, while the femur in the thigh is long and strong so it can carry the body during movements such as running and jumping.

Two Key Parts

The skeleton makes up about a fifth of the weight of an adult's body. It has two key parts. The central part is called the axial skeleton. The other part is called the appendicular skeleton.

The total number of bones in a skeleton is usually 206. The axial skeleton has

The skull, spinal column, ribs, and breastbone make up the axial skeleton (purple). The shoulders, collarbone, pelvis, and limbs make up the appendicular skeleton (green).

A colored X-ray of a ribcage shows how all the bones fit closely together.

Did You Know?

At birth, a baby has more than 300 soft bones. Many of these bones fuse together during childhood. An adult's skeleton has only 206 bones altogether.

A Child's Bones

The bones of a baby are mostly made up of a tough tissue called **cartilage**. The cartilage gradually turns into bone at points called growth plates which are near the ends of the long bones. A good way to make sure your bones are strong and healthy is to be active and eat foods such as dairy products that are rich in **calcium**.

80 bones and the appendicular skeleton has 126. More than half the body's bones are in our hands and feet (see pages 26–27, 29). Most adults have 12 ribs on each side, but one person in 20 has an extra rib.

Inside a Bone

Bones are made of living tissue. This tissue contains fibers called **collagen** and minerals that make the bone strong, including calcium and phosphorus. You also need vitamin D for healthy bones—this vitamin helps the body absorb calcium from food in the intestine and add calcium to your bones.

The Layers of a Bone

A bone has a hard outer layer and a spongy inner layer that looks like a honeycomb. In the middle of long bones such as the femur and some flat bones in the skull, there is a fatty material called bone marrow. A tough skin covers the surface of our bones, except where there is a joint.

The outer layer has lots of rod-shaped structures. Each one has a canal in the middle that carries nerves and blood vessels. Around the canal are layers of collagen that contain tiny spaces. The bone cells here keep the bones healthy and are fed by red bone marrow from the spongy inner layer.

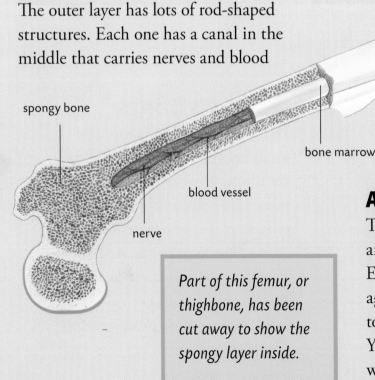

hard bone

spongy bone

bone marrow

blood vessel

nerve

Part of this femur, or thighbone, has been cut away to show the spongy layer inside.

A Lifetime of Growing

The tissue in your bones breaks down and grows again throughout your life. Eventually, when you are around the age of 60, your bone tissue will begin to break down faster than it is made. Your bones will gradually become weaker and less dense.

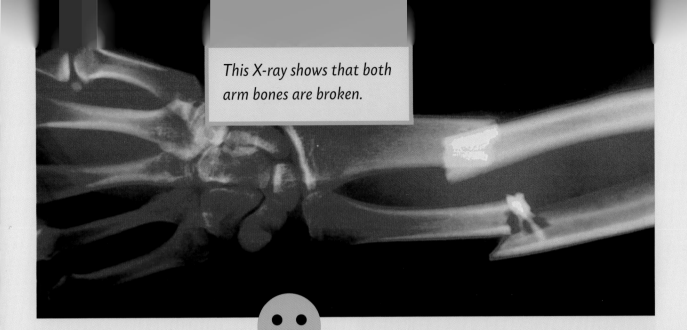

This X-ray shows that both arm bones are broken.

Tricky Repairs

Sometimes a bone breaks awkwardly. The broken parts of the bone need to be held in the right position for the bone to heal properly. This is when you might need a plaster cast around a broken bone to help keep the pieces in position until it is healed.

Bones are very good at repairing themselves. When a bone breaks (or fractures), a clot forms to stop the blood leaking from the damaged blood vessels. The clot is replaced by tissue that gradually grows into spongy bone.

This spongy bone joins the two broken ends back together again. Over several weeks, some of the spongy bone changes into hard bone and this makes the bone strong again.

How a Broken Bone Heals

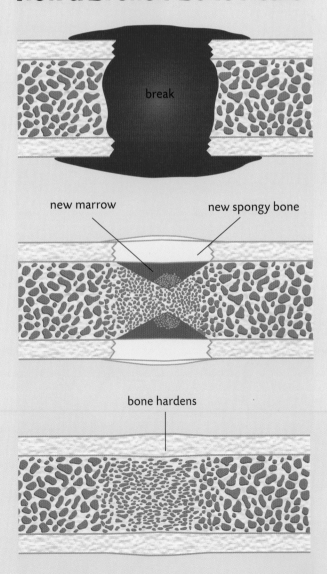

break

new marrow

new spongy bone

bone hardens

Where Bones Meet

Your body can perform an incredible range
of movements, from picking up a pin to jumping high
in the air with your arms spread wide. You can do this
because your bones are connected by flexible joints.
There are several kinds of joints and each one
allows a particular type of movement.

When this tennis player serves, she uses the ball and socket joints in both her shoulders.

Free Movement

Many joints allow the bones they connect
to move in relation to one another. Your
hips, knees, shoulders, elbows, wrists,
ankles, and knuckles are joints that allow
their bones to move freely. They are called
synovial joints. The ends of the bones at a
joint are connected to muscles and are held
in place by strong, stretchy bands of tissue
called **ligaments**.

Some joints, such as those that connect
the bones of the spine, allow just a little
movement. This means the spine can twist
and turn and bend a little, but is also very
stable. A few joints, such as those between
the skull bones, are fused together, which
means they allow no movement at all.

Inside a Joint

The ends of the bones in a synovial joint
are inside a **joint capsule** and they are
covered by a thin layer of cartilage. This
tough tissue protects the bones and helps
them move smoothly over one another.

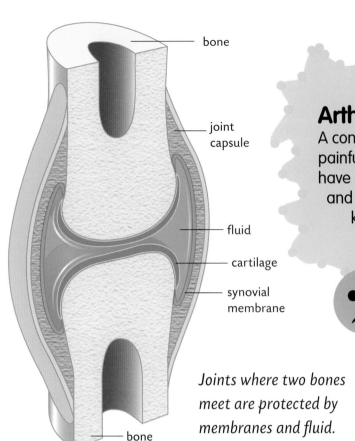

- bone
- joint capsule
- fluid
- cartilage
- synovial membrane
- bone

Joints where two bones meet are protected by membranes and fluid.

The ball and socket joint of the shoulder allows the arm to turn around and move up and down.

A skin called the synovial membrane lines the joint capsule. This releases a layer of slimy liquid called synovial fluid, which stops the bone ends from rubbing together.

Different Joints

There are several types of synovial joints and each one allows a particular kind of movement. Knee, elbow, and finger joints work like the hinges on a door so we can bend and straighten a limb or finger. Hips and shoulders are **ball and socket joints** that can turn in almost any direction.

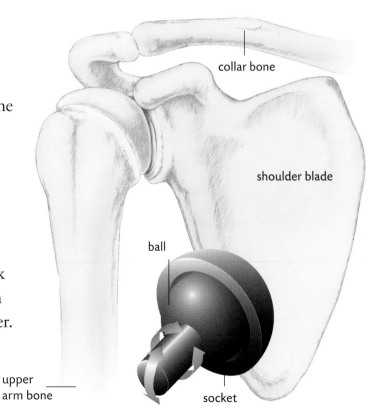

- collar bone
- shoulder blade
- ball
- socket
- upper arm bone

Moving Your Skeleton

More than 600 muscles are attached to the bones of your skeleton. They are called **skeletal muscles** and you use them to move. These muscles are heavy and make up just under half of an adult's body weight.

Skeletal muscles are lots of different sizes. The biggest muscle in your body is called the **gluteus maximus**, which is the main muscle of your bottom. Some of the smallest muscles are those in your hands that allow you to make precise movements with your fingers.

Strong Attachment

Many skeletal muscles cross over a joint and run from one bone to another. Most muscles are wider in the middle than at the ends. Each muscle is joined to a bone by a **tendon**, which is a strong, non-stretchy band of tissue. Some muscles have very long tendons, for example the muscles that move the fingers. Others split and are attached to more than one bone.

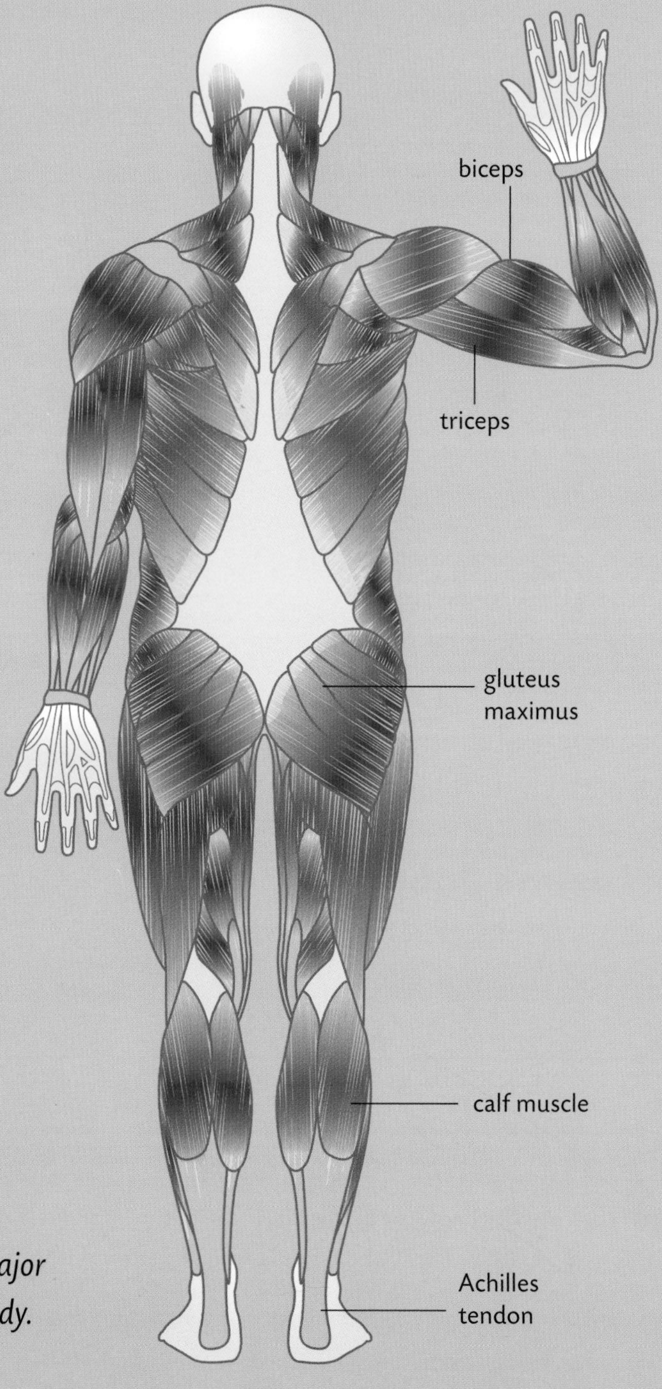

biceps

triceps

gluteus maximus

calf muscle

Achilles tendon

This illustration shows the major muscles in the back of the body.

Muscles form three main layers over your skeleton—these layers are called superficial, intermediate, and deep. They help to form body shape and you can see their outline in people who exercise regularly.

Bundles of Fibers

A skeletal muscle has thousands of tiny muscle fibers inside it. Inside each fiber are smaller fibers called myofibrils running alongside each other. Myofibrils contain thin and thick strands called myofilaments.

When a muscle is relaxed, these filaments lie almost end to end, but when your brain sends them a message, they slide over one another to bunch up in a pile. This makes each myofibril shorter and fatter, so the whole muscle contracts. The filaments lock together when you clench a muscle. When you relax it, they slide apart again and the muscle lengthens again.

This weightlifter needs strength and power, so many of the muscles in his body are big and well-developed, especially the muscles in his arms, shoulders, neck, and thighs.

HUFFING AND PUFFING

When your skeletal muscles work hard during exercise, they use a lot of oxygen, so your heart has to beat faster to pump more blood around your body. This is one reason you breathe more quickly when you are very active, for example when running or playing football. The other reason is that you need to get rid of all the carbon dioxide and other waste that your body is creating.

How Muscles Work

Muscles can contract and shorten, but they can't get longer. This means they pull bones into a new position, but they can't push them. So your muscles work as a pair when they move at a joint—one muscle pulls a bone in one direction and its partner pulls it the opposite way.

Contracting and Relaxing

A pair of muscles works together at the elbow joint. Your upper arm has a muscle called the **biceps** at the front and a muscle called the **triceps** at the back.

When you tighten or contract your biceps muscle, it pulls the forearm up to bend your arm at the elbow. When you contract your triceps muscle, it pulls the forearm down to straighten your arm.

A pair of muscles cannot both contract at the same time. So, when one muscle contracts, its partner relaxes. When the biceps muscle contracts, the triceps muscle relaxes; when the triceps contracts, the biceps relaxes. This happens with all pairs of muscles in the body.

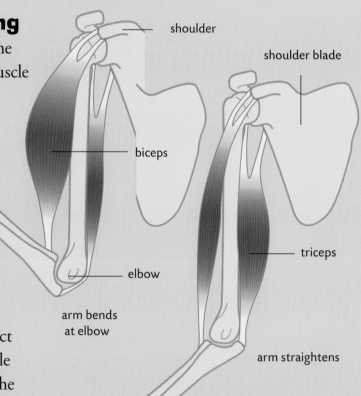

shoulder

shoulder blade

biceps

elbow

arm bends
at elbow

triceps

arm straightens

When the biceps contracts, the arm bends up. When the triceps contracts, the arm straightens.

Holding Your Head Up

Pairs of muscles work with other pairs, so a movement might involve many groups of muscles. A head is heavy—it can weigh 11 lbs (5 kg). To keep it steady, we have layers of strong muscles around the neck and in the upper back. These layers of muscles help keep your head balanced on top of your spinal column. They allow you to move your head from side to side as well as backward and forward (see page 22).

Did You Know?

Your face has 90 muscles. Most are controlled by the facial nerve that branches from your brain. You use about 30 muscles when you change your expression and you use more muscles to frown than to smile.

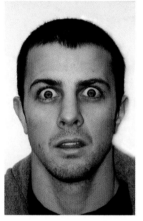

We use a variety of muscles to make different facial expressions.

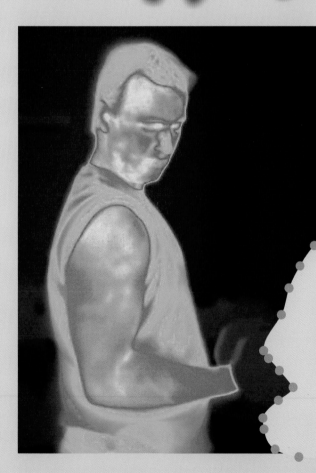

This thermogram shows where heat is produced by a weightlifter. White is hotter than red, and the blue areas are the coldest.

WHEN THINGS GO WRONG

Straining a Muscle

If you stretch a muscle too far, you can damage some of the fibers. This is called a muscle strain and it can happen when you make a sudden movement, perhaps while playing sports. A bad strain can tear the fibers. The best way to avoid muscle strains and tears is to warm up before playing sports.

Staying in Control

You are playing soccer. Your eyes see the ball coming toward you and they help you judge when and where to kick it. Your brain sends messages to the muscles of your leg and foot so you kick the ball at just the right time and in just the right place.

Message System

Every move you make is controlled by your nervous system. Your senses pick up what is going on around you and send messages along nerves to your brain. This then sends messages to your muscles to make the right movement. The messages travel along motor nerves.

Moving in a Pattern

Your brain learns the patterns of movements you repeat again and again. This is why you can do complicated things, such as riding a bike, without thinking about every movement involved.

A piano player doesn't need to think how to move each finger. The player's fingers move in the pattern they have learned while the brain concentrates on reading the music and playing the right notes.

Both automatic and conscious messages control the muscles of someone riding a bike.

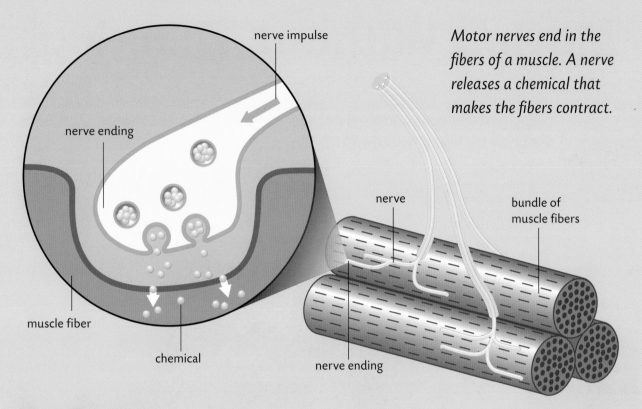

nerve impulse

nerve ending

muscle fiber

chemical

Motor nerves end in the fibers of a muscle. A nerve releases a chemical that makes the fibers contract.

nerve

bundle of muscle fibers

nerve ending

Tiny Sensors

Even when you stand still, you are making small adjustments to your position to hold yourself up and keep your balance. There are tiny sensors in your muscles, ligaments, tendons, and joints. These send information to the brain about where the joints of your body are in relation to one another. The brain continually responds to this information by sending messages to the right muscles to move.

HEALTH CHECK
Test Your Sensors

To find out how well your sensors are working, try the finger-nose test. Hold out one arm at shoulder level, close your eyes, then touch the end of your nose with the first, or index, finger of your other hand. A harder test is to place your index finger of one hand behind your back and then try to touch the tip of it with the index finger of the other hand.

Moving Without Thinking

We consciously control the skeletal muscles that move our bones. But there are two other types of muscles that work without us knowing about it. These are **smooth muscle** and **heart muscle**. Both are controlled automatically by part of the nervous system.

When we eat, automatic muscles take the food to our stomach.

Smooth Muscle

What happens when you have chewed and swallowed a mouthful of food? The food goes down your **alimentary canal**, first to your stomach and then through your intestines. The walls of the alimentary canal are lined with smooth muscle that automatically contracts and relaxes in waves that push the food downwards. This is called **peristalsis**. The large intestine also contains smooth muscle that helps you to push out feces (waste) from your body. Many other parts of the body contain smooth muscle. These include the walls of arteries and the **iris** of the eyes.

Bands of Muscle

There are thick bands of smooth muscle at the ends of some hollow organs and tubes

WHAT MAKES PUPILS BIGGER AND SMALLER?

The colored iris around the pupil of each eye has two kinds of automatic muscle. They control how much light enters your eyes. When the light is bright, the inner muscle contracts and the pupil grows smaller. In dim light, the outer muscle contracts and the pupil grows wider.

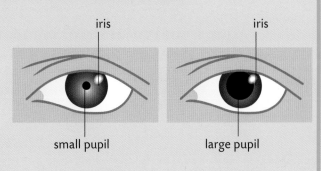

iris   iris

small pupil   large pupil

The pupil (black area) grows smaller in bright light and wider in dim light.

around your body. The bladder has two circular bands called **sphincters**. These contract to keep urine inside your bladder, and then relax to allow it to leave when you have to go. You also have sphincters at the exit of the stomach and the **esophagus**.

Heart Muscle

The walls of your heart contract and relax to pump blood around your body without a rest. The heart (or cardiac) muscle has its own pacemaker that sends tiny electrical messages to contract and relax, unlike skeletal and smooth muscle that rely on the nervous system. The muscle fibers make sure that the four heart chambers contract in the right sequence.

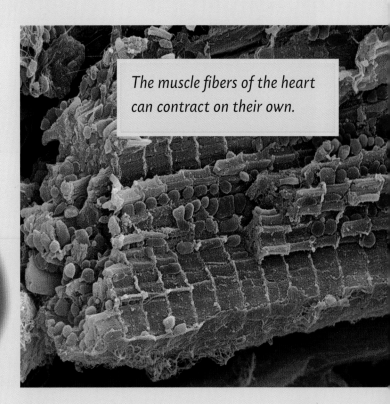

The muscle fibers of the heart can contract on their own.

Did You Know?

Smooth muscle can contract for a long time without taking a rest. It has shorter and thinner muscle fibers than skeletal muscle fibers.

Your Flexible Spine

Your spinal column, or spine, is a long chain of bones that protects the delicate tissue in your spinal cord. The long chain of bones in your spine allows you to bend forward, backward, and sideways. The spine also supports your head.

Groups of Bones

The spine has 33 bones called **vertebrae** that are divided into groups with different names (see page 21). There are seven bones in your neck, twelve behind your chest, five behind your abdomen, and nine in the lower part of the back. The chest vertebrae join to the ribs (see page 24). The nine bones at the bottom are fused so there is no movement between them.

Shock Absorbers

Between the vertebrae are discs of cartilage that help the spine cope with sudden jolts.

Performance gymnasts have amazingly flexible spines.

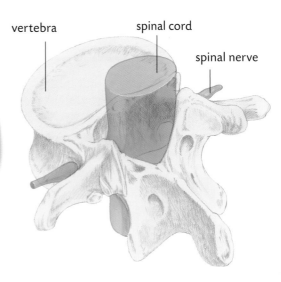

Did You Know?

The discs in your spine are gradually squeezed down through the day and return to their original thickness when you lie in bed at night. That's why you are a tiny bit taller in the morning than you are at night.

Each disc acts as a shock absorber in the same way that shock absorbers in cars or mountain bikes make the ride more comfortable. A disc has a tough outer part around a soft core of jelly-like material.

The spinal cord (green) passes through a hole in the center of each bone (or vertebra) of the spinal column. Spinal nerves branch out of the cord.

The large muscles in your back support your spine and allow it to move in many directions. The individual vertebrae don't move very much but together they make your spinal column very flexible.

Support and Movement

Tough ligaments support the vertebral bones and help to keep your discs in place.

The spinal column has four sections: cervical (red), thoracic (orange), lumbar (yellow), and sacral (green).

WHEN THINGS GO WRONG

A Slipped Disc

If someone puts too much strain on one part of the spine—for example, when lifting a heavy object—part of a disc can bulge outward from between two vertebrae. This is called a slipped disc and it can put pressure on the nerves that branch from the spinal cord, which causes backaches.

Moving Your Head

When you agree with something someone is saying, you nod your head up and down. When you disagree, you turn your head from side to side. Your head is one of the few parts of your body that can move in this way.

Nodding and Turning

Your neck has seven bones, called cervical vertebrae, which start right under your skull. The top bone is called the atlas and the next bone under the atlas is the axis. Two rounded bumps on the base of your skull fit into two dents in the atlas bone. These allow you to move your head up and down with the help of muscles in the front and back of your neck.

The axis bone has a long peg poking up through a hole in the atlas bone above it. This forms a **pivot joint**. You can use different muscles in your neck to turn, or pivot, your head through 180 degrees without moving the rest of your body.

The Skull Jigsaw Puzzle

Your skull has 22 bones that fit together like the pieces of a jigsaw puzzle. The top of the skull is called the cranium and has eight bones. The other 14 bones make up your face. All the bones are fused together to form a rigid structure except your jawbone. This connects to the rest of your skull at two joints on either side.

When you chew, speak, or sing, your jawbone moves up and down. You can also move it from side to side. Your lower teeth are fixed into your jawbone, and your upper teeth are attached to the bone above it.

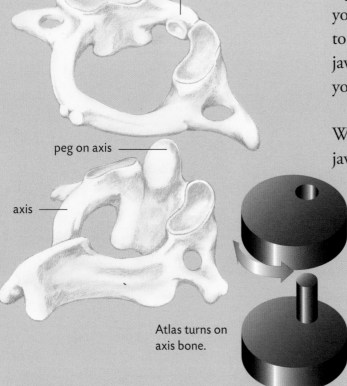

atlas

peg on axis

axis

Atlas turns on axis bone.

The atlas and axis bones at the top of the spinal column allow the head to turn from side to side.

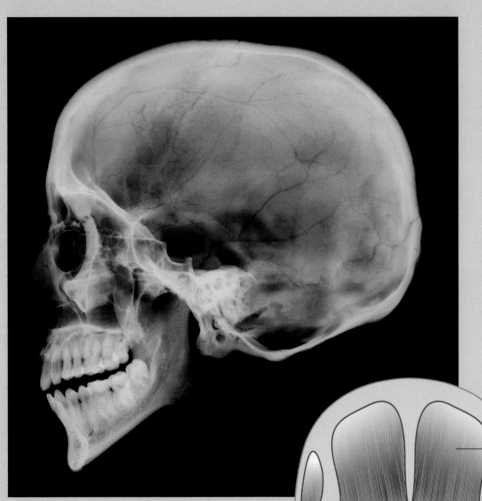

A skull X-ray shows the spaces called sinuses (green, red, and orange areas) inside the head.

forehead muscles

muscles around eye

cheek muscles

lip muscles

chin muscles

AIR HEAD

Your **sinuses** are spaces in your skull that are full of air. They make your skull lighter so it balances easily on top of your spine. The sinuses also make your voice sound clear because they echo sounds formed in your **voice box**. The spaces connect with your nose and have tiny hair-like structures called **cilia** on their lining.

We use our face muscles to blink, chew, kiss, and make expressions (see page 15).

Your Rib Cage and Pelvis

Your rib cage creates a space in your chest
where your lungs expand to breathe in oxygen.
Your pelvis anchors the bottom of your spine
and allows your legs to move.

Breathing Movements

Your rib cage has 12 pairs of ribs attached to 12 bones of the spine at the back. The upper seven ribs on each side are often called the true ribs and they are also attached to the sternum (breastbone) at the front by bands of flexible cartilage. The next few pairs of ribs connect to the cartilage above. Between the ribs are two sets of muscles called **intercostal muscles** and below the ribcage is a thick sheet of muscle called the **diaphragm**. When one set of intercostal muscles and the diaphragm contract, the lungs expand and you breathe in air. When the other set of muscles and the diaphragm relax, you breathe out. The flexible cartilage lets your ribs move up and out as you breathe in.

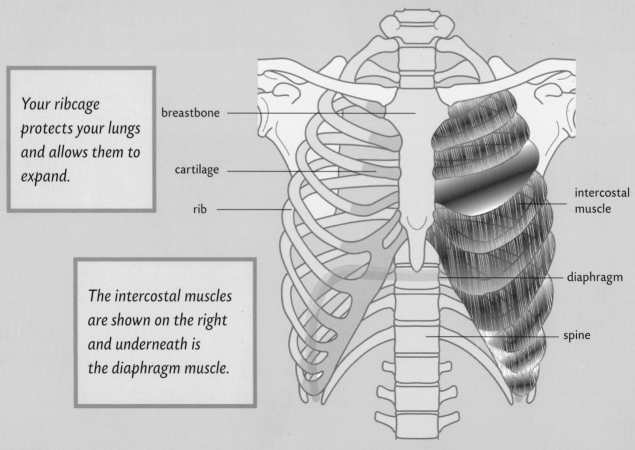

Your ribcage protects your lungs and allows them to expand.

breastbone

cartilage

rib

intercostal muscle

diaphragm

spine

The intercostal muscles are shown on the right and underneath is the diaphragm muscle.

Moving from the Hips

Your pelvis is shaped like a bowl and connects with the top bone, or femur, of each leg inside a ball and socket joint, which is your hip. Your hips allow you to make all kinds of movements with your legs, such as walking, running, kicking, and jumping. Every time you take a step—and you probably take thousands in a day—the ball of the femur turns inside the socket of your hip joint.

All kinds of muscles control the movement of your thigh. You have a very big muscle called the gluteus maximus in each buttock, as well as long muscles that are attached to the knee. These are called the **hamstring** muscles and athletes can tear them when they put too much strain on a thigh.

WHEN THINGS GO WRONG

Needing Hip Replacement

When a hip has been damaged by the wear and tear of arthritis (see page 11), it can be replaced with an artificial one. A surgeon replaces the top of the femur with a metal ball and inserts a metal cup with a very smooth lining into the socket of the pelvis. A new hip can last as long as 15 years.

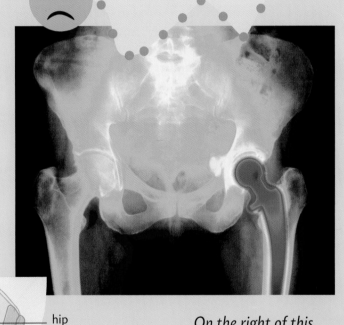

gluteus maximus muscle

hip

ball of thighbone

thighbone

hamstring muscles

thigh straight

thigh lifted

On the right of this X-ray you can see an artificial hip, shown in purple.

Powerful muscles move the ball and socket joint of the hip to lift up the thigh from a straight position.

Skillful Hands

When you write, cut up food, use a computer mouse, or throw a ball, you use the many muscles and bones in your hands. The more you use these muscles and bones, the more things you will be able to do with them.

Flexible Wrists

Your wrists link your hands to your arms. Each wrist has eight bones called **carpal bones**. They are roughly arranged in two rows between the radius bone of your forearm and the bones in the palm of your hand. Your wrists allow your hands to move 360 degrees. You can test this by turning one hand in a circle without moving your forearm (hold the forearm with your other hand to stop it from moving too). Your wrists also allow you to point your fingers in a particular direction. The carpal bones can move together to change what the hand does as a whole or to move a single finger.

The hand has many muscles, tendons, and ligaments that let the fingers and thumbs make small movements.

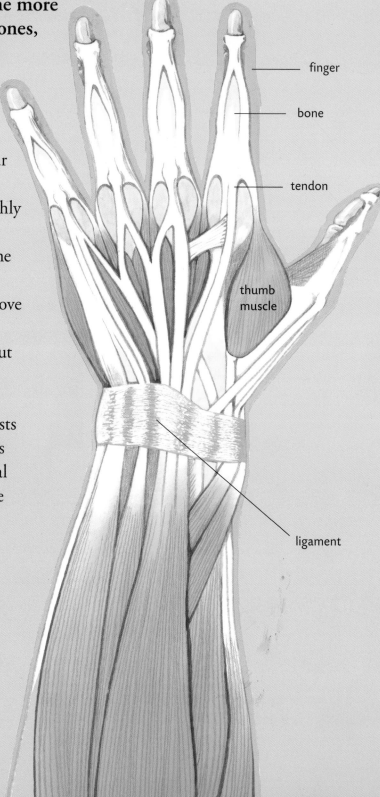

finger

bone

tendon

thumb muscle

ligament

WHEN THINGS GO WRONG

Numb Hand

You can make many movements with your hand and wrist using about 50 muscles in your hand and forearm. Many of these muscles have long tendons that run through tunnels in your wrist. If there is swelling in the main tunnel, pressure on an important nerve can make part of the hand numb or tingly.

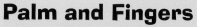

Palm and Fingers

If you look at the back of your hand, you can see five bones that fan out toward your thumb and fingers. These are the slim metacarpal bones of your palm. When you fold your fingers into your palm to make a fist, you create a grip that lets you hold things in your hand.

Each finger has three bones called **phalanges**, which can make very precise movements. The tips of your fingers are very sensitive to touch because they have many nerve endings. Fingers can make very small and precise movements.

The Thumb

The thumb has two phalange bones. It is joined to the first metacarpal bone of the palm by a joint called a saddle joint. The two ends of this joint can move backward and forward over each other and from side to side. They can turn slightly, too.

Humans can touch each fingertip with the thumb of the same hand. This is called having an opposable thumb. It means we can write and use tools. Orangutans and chimpanzees have opposable thumbs on their hands and feet.

The tip of your index finger can touch the tip of your thumb.

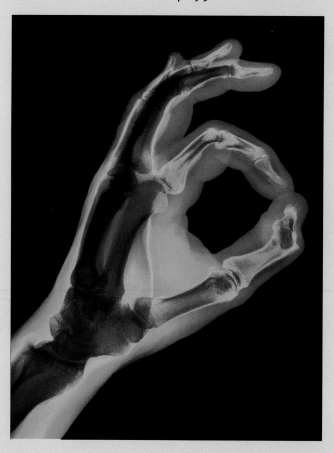

27

Hinged at the Knees

Knees are **hinge joints** like elbows and they let you bend your legs. But knees are more complicated than elbows because they also have to carry the weight of your body. Ankles have the added job of helping to balance your feet on the ground.

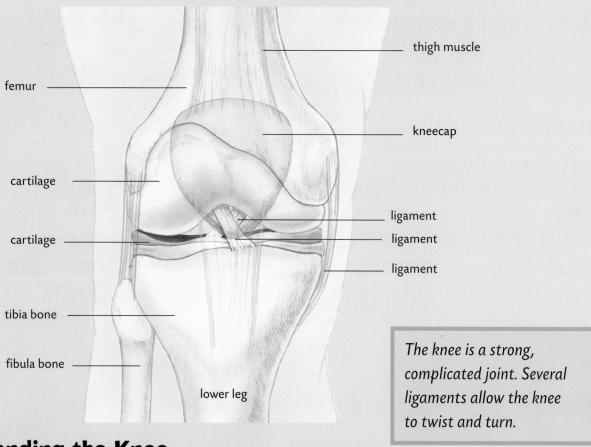

thigh muscle

femur

kneecap

cartilage

ligament

cartilage

ligament

ligament

tibia bone

fibula bone

lower leg

> *The knee is a strong, complicated joint. Several ligaments allow the knee to twist and turn.*

Bending the Knee

Your knee is the joint where the femur, or thighbone, meets the tibia, or shin bone, in the lower leg. The knee has complicated tendons and ligaments outside the joint, and ligaments called cruciate ligaments inside. There are thick pads of cartilage between the lower end of the thighbone and the top end of the shin. These work like shock absorbers and help to make the knee joint stable. The cruciate ligaments and cartilage can tear if the knee is twisted, as can happen when playing ground sports. At the front of the knee you have a small, thick triangular bone called the kneecap, or patella, which helps straighten out your leg.

28

Ankles, Feet, and Toes

Your foot has a similar number of bones to your hand. The ankle has seven tarsal bones and there are five **metatarsal bones** in the arch of each foot. Toes have three phalange bones each and the big toe has two. Your heel is a large bone called the calcaneus bone.

Ligaments hold the bones of your foot and ankle together. These support our feet when we move around and stand still. Layers of muscle bend and straighten your toes and some of these have long tendons.

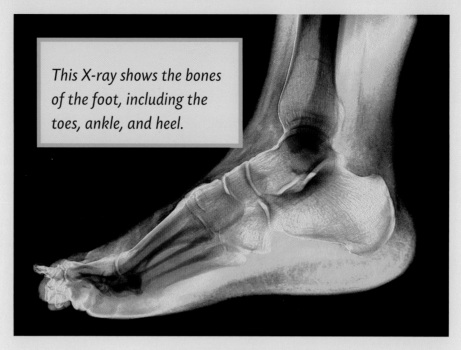

This X-ray shows the bones of the foot, including the toes, ankle, and heel.

GREEK TENDON

At the back of your heel is a large tendon called the Achilles tendon that runs into the main muscle of the calf. If this muscle contracts too quickly or too strongly, the tendon can tear, which makes it impossible to walk. The tendon was named after Achilles, the ancient Greek hero who was famous for his bravery at the Battle of Troy.

Did You Know?

When you walk, you put down the heel of your foot first. Then you move your weight forward to the ball of your foot and finally to your toes, which help you to push off and propel you forward.

Walking involves three stages: 1. putting the heel down, 2. putting the center of the foot down, and 3. putting the toes down.

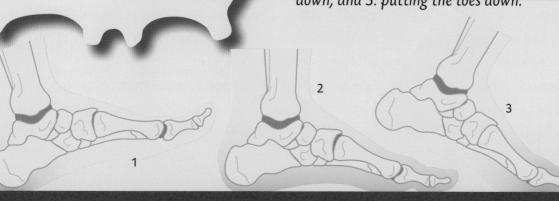

Glossary

alimentary canal   The long tube where we digest food. It starts at the mouth and ends at the anus.

arthritis   A disease that makes joints painful and stiff.

ball and socket joint   A joint such as the hip, where a ball at the end of one bone fits into a socket in another bone.

biceps   The upper arm muscle that bends the arm at the elbow.

bone marrow   A jelly-like substance inside bones.

calcium   A mineral that helps to form bones.

carpal bones   Eight bones in the wrist that allow the hand to turn in different directions.

cartilage   A tough tissue that protects the ends of the bones in a joint. There is cartilage between the bones of the spine and on the tip of the nose.

cilia   Tiny hairs in the lining of the airways of the lungs.

collagen   A type of protein in many parts of the body, such as muscles, tendons, ligaments, and cartilage. Collagen gives strength.

cranium   The main part of the skull around the brain.

diaphragm   The flat, powerful muscle under the lungs that helps them breathe air in and out.

femur   The proper name for the thighbone.

esophagus   Part of the alimentary canal above the stomach.

gluteus maximus   The biggest muscle in the body. Each buttock has a gluteus maximus muscle.

hamstring   A group of muscles in the back of the thigh.

heart muscle   The muscle fibers that form the walls of the heart.

hinge joint   A joint, such as the knee and elbow, that allows a limb to bend or straighten.

intercostal muscles   Muscles between the ribs that allow the ribcage to expand and contract.

iris   The colored part of the eye that controls the size of the pupil.

joint capsule   The protective covering of a synovial joint.

ligaments   Strong, elastic tissue that connects one bone to another.

metatarsal bones   The five long bones that connect the ankle to the toes.

peristalsis   The muscular movement of the esophagus.

phalanges   The bones of the fingers, thumbs, and toes.

pivot joint   The joint at the top of the neck that allows the head to turn from side to side.

sinuses   Air spaces at the front of the skull.

skeletal muscle   Muscles that move the bones of the skeleton.

smooth muscle   Muscles that automatically contract and relax.

sphincter   An opening controlled by smooth muscle.

synovial joints   Joints, such as the knee, where the two bones are protected by a membrane and fluid.

tendon   A tough tissue that joins a muscle to a bone.

triceps   An upper arm muscle that straightens the arm at the elbow.

vertebrae   The bones of the spinal column.

voice box   The structure that holds the vocal cords which vibrate when you speak, sing, or shout.

Further Reading

Muscles (The Amazing Human Body) L.H Colligan, Marshall Cavendish Benchmark, 2010

My Body Mike Goldsmith, Crabtree Publications, 2010

The Mighty Muscular and Skeletal Systems: How do my Bones and Muscles Work? John Burstein, Crabtree Publications, 2009

Web Sites

www.kidsbiology.com/human_biology/skeletal-system.php
Explore the different bones of the body's skeleton.

kidshealth.org/kid/htbw/htbw_main_page.html
Click on "muscle" and "bone" to find out more about how your muscles and skeletal system work.

Index